THE PUMPKIN PIES
AND
THE PUMPKIN PUDDINGS

Story by Paul A. Montuori

Illustrations by Philip Bubbeo

Extra Dessert Publishing

Roslyn Heights, New York

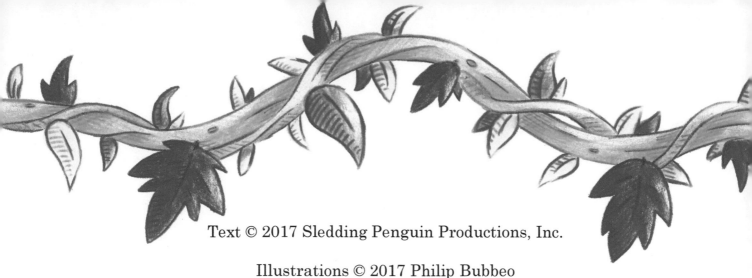

Library of Congress Control Number 2017906911
Montuori, Paul.
The Pumpkin Pies and the Pumpkin Puddings/ Paul Montuori
illustrations by Philip Bubbeo

Copy Editor: Arthur Vidro

ISBN 978-0-9989912-0-7 (hardbound)
ISBN 978-0-9989912-1-4 (softbound)
ISBN 978-0-9989912-2-1 (e-book)

EXTRA DESSERT PUBLISHING

Contact: 246 Mineola Blvd., Suite 109
Mineola, New York 11501

Dedication

To Mom, Granddad and the Family

Thanks for helping me find my way on Stephen's Day

Autumn was always the
most beautiful time of year on the
farm. All the children loved to jump into
the piles of orange and red leaves and
take hayrides after school.

However, it was the middle of October and the pumpkins were getting restless. They were waiting patiently to be picked from the patch and decorated for Halloween.

There was one problem. The local football team was in first place and the whole town was busy cheering them to victory.

GoTEAM!

Everyone forgot
about the poor
pumpkins!

After seeing all the people head to the stadium, the largest of the pumpkins said, "Halloween will soon be here! We don't have much time to waste."

"If everyone is busy watching football games, let's get together and form our own teams." That's how the Pumpkin Pies and Pumpkin Puddings football teams got their start.

The Large Pumpkin assigned each pumpkin to a team. The pumpkins practiced every day.

They passed the ball and
ran up and down the patch.

It was difficult at first for some of the smaller pumpkins, but the bigger pumpkins helped.

The Scarecrow
even pretended he was
announcing the pumpkins'
game on TV!

On the day before Halloween, the Large Pumpkin gathered the teams together and said, "Today is our last chance to be picked."

"When the crowd passes by on the way to the stadium, I'll blow my whistle and we'll begin our football game."

The Pies and Puddings took their positions. All the pumpkins waited eagerly.

When the crowd approached, the
Large Pumpkin blew his whistle.
The game started!

The pumpkins ran and scrambled with the football. The small pumpkins caught the ball and the big pumpkins blocked.

The crowd began to cheer as the pumpkins scored touchdowns. The children said it was the best football game they had ever seen!

Suddenly, the people started running onto the patch to congratulate the pumpkins.

Everyone was so proud of the pumpkins' teamwork. The Pies and Puddings football game became an annual autumn tradition.

The best part was that every pumpkin was picked and decorated for Halloween!

How handsome all the windows in town looked with fancy jack-o'-lanterns lighting the streets, as the children passed by to collect their treats.

When Halloween was through, some of the pumpkins helped make pumpkin pie ...

... and others helped make pumpkin pudding!

NOV
2
THANKSGIVING

CPSIA information can be obtained
at www.ICGtesting.com
Printed in the USA
LVHW070011300922
729649LV00016B/93